W9-CEK-386

LET'S ROCK!

Student protest has turned Miss Glitch's boring Fall Musicale into a rock contest. How can Brother, Sister, and friends compete against groups with trendy names like Girlz, Cyberpunk, and Too-Tall and the Smashers? Only by coming up with a brand-new type of rock.

BIG CHAPTER BOOKS

The Berenstain Bears

GO PLATINUM

by the Berenstains

A BIG CHAPTER BOOK™

Random House New York

www.randomhouse.com/kids
www.berenstainbears.com

Library of Congress Cataloging-in-Publication Data
Berenstain, Stan, 1923–
The Berenstain Bears go platinum / by the Berenstains.
    p. cm. — (A big chapter book)
SUMMARY: The cubs at Bear Country School convince Principal Honeycomb to turn the annual musicale into a rock contest, with a famous heavy metal rock star as judge.
ISBN 0-679-88944-2 (trade). — ISBN 0-679-98944-7 (lib. bdg.)
[1. Rock music—Fiction. 2. Contests—Fiction. 3. Schools—Fiction. 4. Bears—Fiction.] I. Berenstain, Jan, 1923–   . II. Title.   III. Series: Berenstain, Stan, 1923–   Big chapter book.
PZ7.B4483Bejop   1998
[Fic]—dc21   98-17760

Printed in the United States of America   10 9 8 7 6 5 4 3 2 1

BIG CHAPTER BOOKS is a trademark of Berenstain Enterprises, Inc.

Contents

Chapter 1
Musicale

Every fall, not long after the school year started, Bear Country School put on its annual Musicale. The Musicale was the school's biggest annual fundraiser, so everyone—teachers, staff, and students—always felt the need to take part.

Not that they always *wanted* to take part. For many years the Musicale was organized by Miss Glitch, the school's English teacher.

Miss Glitch had very definite ideas about what kinds of music were appropriate for the Musicale. Just two kinds would do, in fact: classical music and folk music—with an emphasis on the *classical*. Her favorite composers were Bearthoven, Schubear, and Sibearius. Now, most cubs didn't *hate* classical music. Some of it was actually pretty good. But it wasn't exactly *their* kind of music, either.

SIBEARIUS   BEARTHOVEN   SCHUBEAR

That's why the Musicale became more popular when Ms. Arpeggio, the pianist, arrived from Big Bear City and took it over. Ms. Arpeggio allowed all kinds of music: not just the newer classical composers like Beartok and Bruvinsky, but also pop music and jazz. Even rock.

Unfortunately, Ms. Arpeggio had never intended to settle in Beartown for the long term. After a couple of years, she got a new job as visiting artist at Big Bear Elementary School in Big Bear City. That put Miss Glitch back in charge of the fall Musicale.

So, this year, when the cubs saw the audition notice for the Musicale posted on the main school bulletin board, they got that old sinking feeling instead of that old excited feeling.

"It won't be the same," said Queenie McBear, looking glumly up at the notice. "Not with Miss Glitch back in charge."

"Cool it," said Brother Bear. "Here she comes now."

Miss Glitch was walking down the hall to her classroom. She saw the cubs gathered in front of the notice and stopped. "I hope I can count on all of you to participate in the Musicale this year," she said brightly.

The cubs just nodded, not really wanting to say anything. But then Queenie blurted out, "Are you going to allow rock bands, the way Ms. Arpeggio did?"

Miss Glitch twisted her face up as if she had just found a disgusting bug clinging to her dress. "I should think not!" she said. "This is a *musicale*. The term 'musicale,' you will notice, contains the word *music*. Your so-called rock music isn't really music. And it all sounds the same, anyway."

"That isn't so!" Queenie protested. "There's all kinds of rock. There's hard rock, classic rock, folk rock, punk rock, alterna-

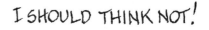

tive rock, country rock, and heavy metal."

"I didn't say there aren't different 'kinds,'" said Miss Glitch. "I said it *all sounds alike.*" And with that, she turned and walked off in the direction of her classroom.

"*I didn't say there aren't different kinds,*" Queenie sneered after Miss Glitch when she was out of earshot. "Boy! She doesn't know *anything!*"

"You don't know everything, either," said Ferdy Factual with one of his famous bored yawns. "You forgot about cyber rock."

"Cyber rock?" said Queenie. "What the heck is that?"

"It's computer rock music," said Trudy Brunowitz, Ferdy's girlfriend. "Harry and Ferdy and I have been experimenting with it."

Harry McGill had just rolled up in his wheelchair. He had the fanciest computer equipment in Beartown and was a real computer whiz. "That's right," he said. "If Ms. Arpeggio were still running the Musicale, we'd be the stars of the show."

"*If* is the main word there," said Sister sadly.

But Queenie didn't look sad. In fact, her eyes were suddenly all asparkle.

"What's with you?" said Brother. "You look like you just got plugged into an electric guitar."

"I've got an idea!" she said. "An idea about how we can *take back the Musicale!*"

6

Chapter 2
Pandora's Rock Box

A couple of mornings later, Miss Glitch barged into the police station and confronted Officer Marguerite at her desk. "I must see Chief Bruno!" she demanded. "Where is he?"

Officer Marguerite looked over her shoulder and said, "He's in his office, Miss Glitch, and the door's open. That means you may go right in."

Miss Glitch marched into Chief Bruno's office. She was carrying three posters, which she slapped down on the chief's desk and spread out for him to see.

"Just look at these!" she said. "They're disgraceful!"

"Hmm," said Chief Bruno, examining the posters. "'*We want rock!' 'Rock lives!' 'Rock forever!*'" Well, I'm not a big fan of rock, Miss Glitch, but I don't see why these are so disgraceful."

"I'll *tell* you why!" said Miss Glitch. "They were put up in place of my posters for the fall Musicale. Which were *torn down!* And it isn't just these three. I put up posters all over town. And they've all been stolen and replaced with 'rock' posters like these! You have to do something, Chief! You have to go after the cubs who did it!"

"I see," said Chief Bruno, leaning back in his swivel chair. "Tell me, Miss Glitch, did you have a permit to put up your posters in town?"

"No," said Miss Glitch. "I didn't think that was necessary."

"Well, it happens to be the law," said Chief Bruno. "And since you put up your Musicale posters illegally, I hardly have an obligation to go after the cubs who took them down and put up these rock posters in their place."

Miss Glitch's face turned red with anger.

Sticking her nose in the air, she marched back out the door, past Officer Marguerite's desk, and out of the station.

Chief Bruno came out of his office. "Hear any of that?" he asked Officer Marguerite.

"How could I miss it?" said Marguerite. "She never closed the door to your office. You sounded like you were ready for her, though."

"I was, sort of," said the chief. "I didn't know about the posters, but my daughter Babs said something last night about all the cubs being up in arms over Miss Glitch not allowing rock music at the Musicale."

Officer Marguerite chuckled. "It sure looks like Ms. Arpeggio opened up Pandora's box when she was here," she said.

"Pandora's *rock* box," said Chief Bruno. "And now poor Miss Glitch can't get the rock back in the box."

Chapter 3
Boycott!

"Well, it's done!" announced Queenie. "We've got the signatures of nearly every cub in the school. Even the kindergartners!"

The cubs were gathered in the schoolyard the next day, waiting for the morning bell. Queenie had a rolled-up paper in her hand. Now she unrolled it. It went all the way down to the ground. At the top it read:

We, the undersigned, vow to boycott the fall Musicale this year if rock music is not allowed. Not only do we refuse to perform in the Musicale, we also refuse to buy tickets to it.

Queenie McBear
Lizzy Bruin
Brother Bear
Sister Bear
Ferdy Factual
Barry Bruin
Babs Bruno
Freddy Bear
Trudy Brunowitz
Too-tall Grizzly
Bonnie Brown
McBear

Beneath that paragraph were at least a hundred signatures. It was easy to tell which of them were the kindergartners'. They were much messier and lumpier than the others.

"What does *boycott* mean, anyway?" asked Barry Bruin.

"Boycott," said Cousin Fred, who read the dictionary for fun. *"To combine in refusing to buy from a store or participate in an activity."*

"I knew that," said Barry.

"Come on, guys," said Queenie. "Let's take this petition to Mr. Honeycomb before school starts."

The cubs marched to the principal's office. Queenie knocked and heard Mr. Honeycomb's voice say, "Come in."

Queenie opened the door to find not just Mr. Honeycomb but also Miss Glitch and Mr. Grizzmeyer, who doubled as vice principal and sports coach. "Sorry, Mr. Honey-comb," said Queenie. "We didn't mean to interrupt..."

"It's all right," said the principal. "What have you got there?"

Queenie let the petition unroll all the way to the floor again. "We want rock music at the Musicale," she said. "And so do most of the other students."

Brother said, "That's right," and Sister said, "You tell 'em, Queenie!" The other cubs all nodded.

"Well, now," said Mr. Honeycomb. "It so happens that Miss Glitch, Mr. Grizzmeyer, and I were just discussing that very issue. And I was saying that in view of the fact that so many cubs are in favor of including rock music in the Musicale, it seems only fair to compromise."

"Compromise?" said Queenie. "What do you mean?"

"Well," said Miss Glitch, "I'll agree to allow rock music in the Musicale if some rock group will promise to perform at least one of my favorite pieces."

"Which are?" said Queenie.

" 'The Bear Danube Waltz,' 'The Bear Country National Anthem,' and 'The Bear Spangled Banner,' " said Miss Glitch.

The cubs let out a group groan.

"And another group can perform *my* favorite song," said Mr. Grizzmeyer.

"What is it?" asked Queenie.

"The school fight song, of course," said Mr. Grizzmeyer. "Which *I* wrote."

Just then a foursome at the back of the group of cubs belted out the fight song:

It was Too-Tall and his gang, who now pushed their way to the front of the group.

"Bravo!" said Mr. Grizzmeyer. "How about *you* guys doing the song at the contest?"

"No disrespect, Coach, but no way," said Too-Tall. "I've got a completely different idea."

"This is outrageous!" protested Miss Glitch. "Allowing these ruffians to barge right in—"

"Now wait a second, Miss Glitch," said Mr. Honeycomb. "These ruffians have just as much right to speak as the other cubs. Go ahead, Too-Tall."

"Thanks, Mr. H," said Too-Tall. "You're an okay guy. Now let me ask you all a question. What exactly is the purpose of the annual Musicale?"

"To foster the love of music in the student population," said Miss Glitch.

"To build cubs' character by forcing them to perform before a large audience," said Mr. Grizzmeyer.

"And to raise money for Bear Country School," added Mr. Honeycomb.

"All good answers," said Too-Tall. "Now let's examine those purposes. *Love of music.* Some bears love classical music, others love rock music. *Performing before an audience.* That fits both classical and rock. But what about *raising money?* I say that *rock* music is where the money is. If you wanna raise money, you shouldn't just *include* rock in the Musicale. You should make it an all-rock concert. In fact, you should go one step further and turn it into a rock *contest!* Ticket sales would go through the roof!"

The cubs buzzed with excitement as Mr. Grizzmeyer and Miss Glitch grumbled with displeasure. Mr. Honeycomb finally signaled for quiet.

"Too-Tall," he said, "I almost hate to admit it, but you might be onto something there."

"Mr. Honeycomb!" gasped Miss Glitch. "You can't *mean* that!"

"Forget the fight song, Mr. H," said Mr. Grizzmeyer. "I was only kidding—"

"Now, wait," said Mr. Honeycomb. "May I remind you two what the Musicale is raising money for? Programs not fully funded in the school budget. That includes the *music* program, Miss Glitch. And, Mr. Grizzmeyer, it also includes the *sports* program. The music program, I might add, covers the school orchestra, which will be performing works this year by your beloved Bearthoven and Schubear, Miss Glitch. Of course, that particular concert may have to be canceled if the Musicale doesn't raise enough money. And the sports program includes your beloved wrestling team, Mr. Grizzmeyer, which might have to cut its schedule due to lack of funds."

For a moment there was utter silence in Mr. Honeycomb's office. Then Miss Glitch said, "All right, Mr. Honeycomb. I give up. A rock contest it is."

A cheer started to build among the cubs, but Mr. Honeycomb raised a hand to quiet them. He turned to the vice principal. "What do you say, Mr. G?" he said. "We'd

very much like to proceed with your bless-
ing."

Mr. Grizzmeyer had been gnashing his
teeth. Now he let his jaw relax and heaved a
deep sigh. "Let's rock," he said softly.

The cubs cheered loud and long.

Chapter 4
Toxic Sludge

Later that afternoon Brother, Sister, Fred, Lizzy, and Bonnie Brown were walking home from school. All day, school had been buzzing with excitement about the rock contest. Rumors had been flying all over the place about who would enter and what kinds of bands they would come up with. But until now, no one had thought to ask one very interesting question.

"Hey," said Fred suddenly, "how do you suppose Too-Tall came up with the idea for a rock contest, anyway? I mean, when has *he* ever been concerned about raising money for the school?"

"Hmm," said Brother. "Now that you mention it, I can think of just one reason Too-Tall would want to turn the Musicale into a rock contest. He thinks he has a sure-fire way of winning."

The others nodded in agreement.

They were right, too. For at that very moment, Too-Tall and his gang were gathered in their clubhouse out behind Two-Ton Grizzly's Parts R Us lot, talking about Too-Tall's plan.

"So, what's your idea, boss?" said Skuzz. "I've been dyin' to hear it."

"Simple," said Too-Tall. He waved a hand at the walls of the clubhouse. They were covered with Toxic Sludge posters. Toxic Sludge was Too-Tall's favorite rock band. It was famous for its weird outfits, weird hairdos, and even weirder onstage behavior. At the start and end of each performance, the band smashed a set of electric guitars to smithereens.

"Huh?" said Vinnie, frowning at the posters. "You want Toxic Sludge to stand in for us?"

Too-Tall rapped on Vinnie's forehead with his knuckles. "Hello? Anybody home? We do an act like theirs, dummy. We can call ourselves Too-Tall and the Smashers."

"I still don't get it, boss," said Vinnie. "Do you mean we're gonna smash our electric guitars? What'll old Glenn Clef say?" Glenn Clef owned the music store where the gang had recently bought their secondhand guitars and a secondhand drum set.

"He's right for once, boss," said Smirk. "Those guitars ain't even paid up yet."

"Besides," said Skuzz, "how would we replace them? We ain't got the dough."

"Quit yer whinin'," said Too-Tall. "I got it all worked out. Remember when I took Mr. Hammer aside in shop class this afternoon? I was askin' him if we could make a bunch

26

of fake guitars out of plywood over the next couple weeks. And he said okay."

"Fake guitars?" said Vinnie. "We're gonna smash our real guitars and play fake ones? That ain't gonna work, boss."

Skuzz and Smirk chuckled as Too-Tall put his arm around Vinnie's shoulders and leaned down to whisper in his ear. "We play our *real* guitars, bonehead. We smash the *fake* ones. Four at the start of the act, and four at the end."

"Cool!" said Vinnie. "Just like Toxic Sludge!"

"There ya go, Vin," said Too-Tall. "I always said you've got a mind like a steel trap."

"Yeah," snickered Smirk. "He just doesn't oil it enough!"

Cautiously, Skuzz raised his hand. "Er, uh...boss?"

"What is it, Skuzzbrain?" said Too-Tall.

28

"I know how much you love Toxic Sludge," said Skuzz. "Heck, I love 'em, too. But grownups *hate* 'em. And Mr. Honeycomb already announced that he's gonna appoint two *teachers* to judge the contest. So how we gonna win?"

Too-Tall smiled. "Don't worry," he said. "I'm workin' on that, too."

Chapter 5
Smashing Bananas

A couple of evenings later, Brother and Sister were watching BMTV—Bear Music Television—in their living room after dinner. Papa came in and plopped down in his easy chair. He held out his hand. "Remote," he said.

"But, Papa!" whined Sister, snatching the

remote from Brother and clutching it to her chest. "We're watching Toxic Sludge! They're the hottest rock band in Bear Country!"

"Toxic Sludge?" said Papa. "What kind of stupid name is that?"

"Didn't you have a favorite band when *you* were young?" asked Brother.

"Sure," said Papa. "It was Bruin Brown and His Band of Renown."

"Bruin Brown and His Band of Renown?" said Sister. "What kind of stupid name is *that?*"

But Papa didn't even hear her. He was staring in horror at the TV as Toxic Sludge went into its act-ending destruction of guitars. "They're smashing their guitars to pieces!" he said. "Are they quitting the business?"

"Oh, Papa," said Brother. "They do that every time they sing. It's part of their act."

"It is?" said Papa. "That must cost them a whole lot of money!"

"Less than they make in ten seconds of performing," said Brother. "I think Too-Tall and his gang are gonna imitate them in the big contest. I saw them making plywood guitars in shop class today. Perfect for smashing."

"Makes a lot more sense than smashing expensive *electric* guitars," said Papa. "Not that any of it makes any sense." He held out his hand again. "Remote."

"But, Papa!" said Sister, clutching the remote more tightly. "Smashing Bananas is gonna sing now! Look, here they come!"

Three very skinny bears appeared on the screen, each with spiky, multi-colored hair. They were wearing banana necklaces. *Real* bananas hooked to gold chains.

"Smashing Bananas?" said Papa, staring. "Why are they called Smashing Bananas?"

"Because at the end of their act they smash all the bananas," said Brother matter-of-factly.

"Ask a silly question, get a silly answer," said Papa.

"No, I'm serious," said Brother.

"Hmm," said Papa as Smashing Bananas began to make their guitars screech and whine. "Sounds pretty serious to me, too."

After a few ear-shattering minutes of guitars shrieking and moaning, not to mention the screaming of the lead singer, the group plucked bananas from their gold chain necklaces and smashed them on their instruments. Then they smashed some more on *each other's* instruments. Then they smashed some more all over their own bodies. And, finally, they smashed the rest all over *each other's* bodies.

"Cool!" said Brother.

"Awesome!" breathed Sister.

Smashing Bananas took their bows and blew banana-smeared kisses to their adoring fans. Their bodies, their instruments, and the entire stage were lathered with oozing banana pulp.

"Gee," said Papa. "I wonder if they've

ever considered starting a baby food business." He rose and headed upstairs. "I think I'll go look for some of my old Bruin Brown and His Band of Renown records."

Sister rolled her eyes at Brother. "What is it about grownups?" she said. "They don't seem to understand *anything!*"

"I heard that," said Mama, coming in from the kitchen. "Don't be too hard on Papa. He understands lots of things. He just doesn't understand the music you cubs like nowadays."

"Do you?" asked Sister.

"Hardly," Mama admitted. "But I also remember how *my* folks didn't understand the music *I* liked as a cub. Say, are you two going to enter the big rock contest?"

"Sure," said Brother. "With Fred, Lizzy, and Bonnie."

"What kind of a group will it be?" Mama wanted to know.

"We haven't really decided yet," said Brother. "Most of the categories are already taken. Too-Tall and the gang are probably going to imitate Toxic Sludge—that's heavy metal. Queenie and Bermuda McBear and Babs Bruno have a group called Girlz that does feminist rock. Harry McGill, Ferdy Factual, and Trudy Brunowitz are doing cyber rock with Harry's fancy computer equipment. And Barry Bruin is mixing rock with stand-up comedy."

"Can't you enter a band in one of those same categories?" asked Mama.

"Sure," said Brother. "But those groups are gonna be really good—except for Barry's, of course. There's only one prize, and if we want a chance to win it, we have to come up with something different."

"We're thinking of country rock," said Sister.

"Country?" said Mama. "You mean like

Loretta Grizz?"

"No, Mama!" scoffed Sister. "Country
rock. Like Garth Bruin."

"Who?"

"Never mind," said Sister.

"Well, that all sounds very nice," said Mama. "You could borrow Grizzly Gran's washboard and old one-bear-band instruments. And Gramps's jug."

"You mean an old-fashioned *jug* band?" gasped Sister.

"Sure," said Mama. "Why not? Gramps and Gran could coach you."

Brother laughed. "Hey, Sis," he said. "What's more uncool: entering a jug band in a rock contest or having your *grandparents* coach you?"

Sister put a hand to her chin and pretended to think really hard. "It's a toss-up," she said finally.

Mama realized she had been just a little off the mark with her suggestion. But she had always loved jug bands. "Well," she said, "it wouldn't have to be a real jug band.

You could use Gramps and Gran's old instruments *with* your electric guitars. It would certainly be different, wouldn't it?"

Brother rolled his eyes. "No kidding," he said.

"Thanks a million, Mama," said Sister. "We'll think about it."

The cubs wasted no time in turning their full attention back to BMTV.

Chapter 6
The Announcement

Of course, Brother and Sister were only kidding when they said they'd think about Mama's suggestion. But the very next day, something happened at school that actually did make them think about it.

As the cubs settled into their classrooms for the morning, they heard Mr. Honeycomb's voice on the public-address system. He announced that he was naming Teacher Bob and Miss Glitch as judges of the big rock contest. Later, at morning recess, Brother and Sister's rock group met on the playground to discuss what the announcement meant for the contest.

"It's a disaster!" moaned Sister. "*Miss Glitch?* Gimme a break!"

"Teacher Bob's bad enough," grumped Lizzy.

"Now, hold on," said Bonnie. "There's hope for Teacher Bob. He may not be familiar with modern rock, but I happen to know he likes *classic* rock. He owns every album ever made by the Beartles and the Rolling Bones."

"But what about Miss Glitch?" said Sister. "She can't tell the difference between Toxic Sludge and Pond Scum!"

"Sure, she can," said Fred, with a twinkle in his eye. "Pond scum is green, and toxic sludge is black."

"You wanna make jokes?" snapped Sister. "Go join *Barry's* band!"

"Calm down, Sis," said Brother, putting an arm around her shoulders. "All the *other* groups are hurt just as much by this as ours."

"Not!" said Sister. "Miss Glitch is bound

to go for Ferdy's cyber rock group. She *loves* nerds!"

"Did someone call me?" asked Ferdy, approaching with Trudy at his side. "I couldn't help overhearing. Sister is quite correct. Miss Glitch being named a judge of the contest clearly favors our band."

"*Cyber rock*," sneered Sister. "They should call it *nerd* rock! That stuff is just *too* weird. I think they should only allow bands from *Planet Earth* in the contest."

"Hmm," said Ferdy, turning to Trudy. "*Nerd rock*. I like the sound of that, don't you?"

"Maybe we should change the name of our group from Cyberpunk to Nerd Rock," joked Trudy as she and Ferdy walked off.

Fred stared after them. "Just look at those two," he said. "Now their SQs are as high as their *IQs*."

"SQs?" said Bonnie.

"Smugness Quotients," said Fred. "They're the front runners now, for sure."

But Brother had a doubtful look on his face. "Don't be so sure," he said. Then his eyes widened, as if an idea had just come to him. "Hey, Sis, remember what Mama said last night?"

"You mean about a jug band?" said Sister, frowning. "Are you sure you're feeling all right?"

"Now hear me out," said Brother. "Miss Glitch may love nerds, but she also loves *tradition*. What could be more traditional than an old-fashioned jug band?"

"But a jug band's not even a rock band!" protested Sister.

"Mama suggested *combining* rock instruments with jug band instruments," Brother pointed out. "It could be a lot of fun. And we'd be inventing a completely new kind of country rock!"

"*Jug rock?*" said Fred.

"Sure!" said Bonnie. "And we can give the band an old-fashioned-sounding name. Like 'the Jugsters.' Miss Glitch'll love it. And Teacher Bob'll probably go for it, too."

Sister shook her head. "Is *winning* all you guys care about?" she said.

"Look," said Brother. "We've already decided on country rock. We can do an old-fashioned country song and put it to a rock beat."

"Yeah," said Bonnie. "Like 'My Flaky Breaky Heart.' "

"We can use Gramps and Gran's instru-

JUG ROCK?

ments," said Brother, "and they can coach us, just like Mama said."

Bonnie, Lizzy, and Fred were all for it. But Sister was still wavering. Finally she said, "I'll agree to it on one condition: that we don't tell anyone where we got the instruments or who taught us how to play them. *Or* where the idea came from."

The others looked at one another in surprise. "Absolutely!" said Brother. "Do you think we're *crazy?*"

Chapter 7
A Most Surprising Letter

It seemed as if Miss Glitch's appointment as rock-contest judge doomed the chances of Too-Tall's band. His gang certainly thought so. But not Too-Tall. Whenever his buddies started bemoaning the appointment, he would say, "Quit whinin', morons!" But he'd say it in a joky, good-natured way, not angrily. The gang began to wonder if he knew something they didn't. Why, for example, was he going home every afternoon before school finished to check the mail?

Then, one afternoon, Too-Tall came barging through the door of the clubhouse, waving a piece of paper in the air. Moments before, he had hurried off to the Grizzly home on Two-Ton's Parts R Us lot to check the mail.

"It finally came!" he cried. "He's gonna do it!"

"What're ya talkin' about, boss?" said Skuzz. "Who's gonna do what?"

Too-Tall took a deep breath and tried to get ahold of himself. "Remember when you guys were complaining about how teachers were gonna judge the contest?" he said. "And I said I was workin' on it? Well, I knew that Toxic Sludge was gonna be performing in Big Bear City right around the time of the contest, so I wrote 'em and asked 'em if they'd come judge our contest. And the lead singer just wrote back and said he *would!*"

The gang stared in awe at the letter in Too-Tall's hand.

"You mean Toxic Ted is gonna judge the

contest?" gasped Vinnie.

"No, half-wit!" growled Too-Tall. "He's the drummer! I said the lead singer!"

"Stevie Sludge!" cried Smirk. "That's fantastic!"

"Yeah," said Skuzz. "Except for one thing, boss. Teacher Bob and Miss Glitch are already the judges!"

"*Were* the judges, you mean," said Too-Tall. He glanced at his watch. "It's afternoon recess time at school. Let's go start a revolution!"

"Go to school?" whined Vinnie. "I thought we were playin' hooky today, boss."

"Sure, we were," said Too-Tall, patting Vinnie on the back. "But now we got a *reason* to go to school!"

Chapter 8
Sludge Mania

Too-Tall and the gang ran to the schoolyard and started showing the letter around. Within minutes they had all the cubs on the playground behind them—even the other rock bands. The news of Stevie Sludge's

decision was so thrilling that all the maneuvering and politicking about how to win the contest went right down the drain. Too-Tall was an instant hero.

Along with Girlz and the Jugsters, Too-Tall and the Smashers marched straight to Mr. Honeycomb's office and presented the letter to him. "Mr. H," said Too-Tall, "this is absolutely the best thing that could have happened to our rock contest!"

Frowning, Mr. Honeycomb read the letter. Then he looked up at the cubs and asked, "What in the world is Toxic Sludge?"

The cubs let out a collective gasp. Their principal had never heard of Toxic Sludge!

"They're a famous rock group!" said Too-Tall.

"Heavy metal," said Queenie. "Sort of halfway between Toenails and Pond Scum."

"Toenails?" said Mr. Honeycomb. "Pond Scum?"

"They're more rad than Hairball," explained Brother, "but not as rad as Stinking Violet."

"Hairball?" said Mr. Honeycomb. "Stinking Violet?"

It was no use explaining. Mr. Honeycomb had never heard of *any* of the new rock groups. But although he was ignorant about Toxic Sludge, he wasn't dead set against the group. He told the cubs that he would call a meeting of the whole faculty to discuss the letter from Stevie Sludge.

Some of the teachers, on the other hand, were *not* ignorant about Toxic Sludge. And they couldn't have been deader set against Stevie Sludge judging the contest than if he had been the Devil himself. Especially Mr. Grizzmeyer and Miss Glitch. "We mustn't let that disgusting radical come anywhere *near* Bear Country School!" exclaimed Miss Glitch when Mr. Grizzmeyer told her about the letter. Together they planned a two-pronged attack.

At the faculty meeting, Mr. Grizzmeyer was the first to present his case. He passed around some photos of Toxic Sludge.

Mr. Honeycomb expressed shock at their frightening, grungy appearance, especially their hideously painted faces and spiky hair. But Teacher Bob pointed out that they didn't look any grungier than Mr. Hyde had looked in the classic movie *Dr. Bruin and Mr. Hyde*. Nor were they more frightening than the monster in *Frankenbear*. The principal was forced to admit that Teacher Bob had a point.

Miss Glitch was confident that the second prong of the attack would do the necessary damage. She rose and said, "It isn't just their appearance that we object to. Their language is foul and disgusting! Not to mention *ungrammatical*. Just listen..." She placed a Toxic Sludge CD in the boom box she'd brought with her, turned the volume all the way up, and pressed the *PLAY* button.

When the screeching, wailing tones of Toxic Sludge had at last faded away, it took the assembled faculty a few moments to unclench their teeth.

"It's kind of like getting hit over the head with a sledgehammer," commented

Mr. Smock, the art teacher.

"Don't you mean a *Sludge* hammer?" cracked Teacher Jane.

"I agree with you completely about their music," said Mr. Honeycomb. "But since you can't understand a single word they're saying, I don't see what harm their language can do."

Most of the teachers murmured their agreement.

"I might add," continued the principal,

"that ticket sales for the contest jumped as soon as word got around that Mr. Sludge will attend. If we make him a *judge,* I daresay sales will go through the roof." He turned to Mr. Grizzmeyer. "That would mean not only will your wrestling team have a full schedule this year, but the basketball team can get the new uniforms you asked for." He turned next to Miss Glitch. "And it would also mean that the orchestra can travel to Big Bear City and take part in the Bear Country School Orchestra Festival later this year."

Once more, Mr. Grizzmeyer and Miss Glitch found themselves between a rock and a hard place. The rock of Toxic Sludge, so to speak, and the hard place of insufficient funds for their favorite school programs.

And that's how Stevie Sludge got to judge the Bear Country School Rock Contest.

Chapter 9
Dress Rehearsal

As soon as it was announced that Stevie Sludge would judge the rock contest, ticket sales did indeed go through the roof. Right through the roof of the school auditorium

and into Great Grizzly Hall. It was clear that the audience would be too large for the auditorium, so the contest was moved to Beartown's main concert hall.

"This is fantastic!" Teacher Bob told Mr. Honeycomb when the move was decided. "The school will make a fortune! We'll go platinum!"

"Excuse me, Teacher Bob," said the principal, "but what exactly does *platinum* have to do with the situation?"

Sister and Brother happened to overhear as they passed in the hall. "Why is it that grownups don't know *anything?*" Sister asked Brother, who just shrugged.

Although the contest was moved to Great Grizzly Hall, the dress rehearsal was still held in the school auditorium. Papa drove Brother and Sister to it, and on the way he played his tape of Bruin Brown and His Band of Renown. The cubs were so polite about it that they made only one comment. That was when Sister said, "You'd better stop the car, Papa, 'cause I think I'm gonna throw up."

Sister felt much better when they got to the auditorium and saw the huge speakers and strobe lights that had been loaned to the contest by BMTV, which was owned by Squire Grizzly, Bonnie Brown's uncle. Not to mention the winner's prize, set off to one side of the room. It was a big statue of a

smashed guitar, sculpted by Mr. Smock.

"That's a prize only a rock fan could love," said Papa as he set down the heavy carrying case that contained Gran's old one-bear-band set.

"Well, *I'm* a rock fan, and I love it!" said Sister. "Now, go get the jug, Papa."

Gramps's big ol' jug was so heavy that Sister made Papa lug it wherever it needed to be lugged. She played it in the band while Brother played the one-bear-band set and Lizzy played the washboard. Bonnie and Fred played the electric guitars.

When Papa got back with the jug, Barry Bruin's group, the Stand-ups, were about to begin their act. The audience consisted of the competing bands.

"And now we'd like to perform a brand-new kind of rock for you," Barry announced. "It's like heavy metal, but lighter. We call it 'heavy metal lite.'" He paused to give the audience a chance to laugh. No one laughed. " 'Aluminum?' " he said. Still no laughs.

"I'm outta here," said Papa, holding his nose. "Be back later."

After Papa left, the Stand-ups didn't get any better. Their act consisted of bad music interrupted by a series of even worse jokes.

"Well, I guess that puts the Stand-ups out of the running," gloated Fred as Barry and his group made way for Girlz.

"The Stand-ups were never *in* the running," scoffed Brother.

As Girlz launched into their original rendition of the old feminist favorite "I Am Female," Too-Tall and the Smashers

entered the auditorium and made their way to the row of seats behind the Jugsters.

"What did we miss?" asked Too-Tall.

"Just the Stand-ups," said Brother over his shoulder.

"In other words," said Fred, "*nothing*."

Sister noticed that Too-Tall and his gang hadn't brought any instruments. "Hey," she said, "aren't you guys gonna rehearse?"

"Nah," said Too-Tall. "We could only do part of our act, anyway."

"Why's that?" asked Fred, winking at Brother.

"'Cause if we did the whole act in rehearsal," said Too-Tall, "we'd only have part of it left to do at the contest. You'll see what I'm talkin' about at the contest."

Fred nudged Brother and said, "Guess that confirms your theory about why they've been making those plywood guitars in shop class."

"Right," said Brother. "And I'll bet it ties into why Too-Tall was so hot to get Toxic Sludge to judge the contest. You know what it all means, don't you?"

"Sure," said Fred. "It means that Too-Tall and the Smashers are gonna win the contest."

But neither he nor Brother was so sure of that when Cyberpunk replaced Girlz on the stage. It took a small crew of moving bears to bring in Harry McGill's computer equip-

ment from their pickup truck. The group wore costumes with an outer-space theme. There were no vocals to their music, which consisted mainly of a lot of weird moans and trills. The most impressive part came at the end when the three players alternated, imitating and embellishing each other's sound creations.

"Wow," said Skuzz when they were done. "Pretty spaced out, huh, boss?"

"They could be our main competition," said Too-Tall. "And they already got past the censors."

"What censors?" said Smirk.

"Miss Glitch and Mr. Grizzmeyer have to pass all the song lyrics for the contest," said Too-Tall. "I handed ours in today. They're gonna rule on 'em tomorrow."

"But these Cyberpunks don't *have* any lyrics, boss," said Vinnie.

"That's my point, bonehead!" said Too-Tall.

"They're home free. I'm worried about 'em. Stevie Sludge might like 'em. Come on, let's get outta here."

"Hey," said Brother as Too-Tall and the gang rose to leave. "Aren't you gonna stay to hear the Jugsters?"

Too-Tall laughed. "The Jugsters?" he said. "Gimme a break. We came to check out the competition. The Jugsters ain't *competition*. Not with Stevie Sludge judgin' the contest."

"Ain't it the truth, boss?" said Skuzz.

"When Stevie Sludge takes one look at that ugly ol' jug and that crazy one-bear-band set, he's gonna fall right off his chair laughin'!"

"Where did you guys get those dumb instruments, anyway?" said Smirk. "And who taught you to play 'em?"

"Don't bother tellin' us," said Vinnie with a wink. "'Cause we already know. *Gramps and Gran!*"

The gang did a lot of laughing of their own as they strutted toward the exit. Brother and Sister started hauling the jug up onto the stage, while Bonnie and Fred hefted the one-bear-band carrying case. But by the time they had everything set up, they found themselves all alone in the auditorium. All the other bands had left.

It was beginning to look as if the Stand-ups weren't the only group that was "out of the running."

Chapter 10
Sense and Censorship

The next morning Mr. Honeycomb met with Mr. Grizzmeyer and Miss Glitch in his office to approve the song lyrics for the contest.

"First on the list is the Stand-ups," said Mr. Honeycomb, turning to their lyrics. "They're performing a number called 'Take My Mom...Please!' " He began to read the lyrics aloud: " 'Ladies and germs. I just flew in from Big Bear City. Boy, are my arms tired!' " He looked at the others. "These are song lyrics? There must be some mistake..."

Miss Glitch explained the nature of the Stand-ups' act. Mr. Honeycomb turned to the lyrics of "I Am Female" by Girlz.

"'I am female, hear me roar!

G-R-R-R-R-R-R-R!' "

"Is that it?" said Mr. Grizzmeyer. "It doesn't make sense!"

"They're rock lyrics, for heaven's sake," said Miss Glitch. "They're not *supposed* to make sense. But I would like to point out, Mr. Honeycomb, that the word 'Girlz' is misspelled. We'll have to correct that for the program notes."

Mr. Honeycomb assured her that the misspelling was on purpose and turned to the lyrics for Too-Tall and the Smashers.

"'Down with mush, down with love!

Up with push, up with shove!

Down with neat, down with clean!

Up with dirt, up with mean!' "

"I object!" said Miss Glitch. "Those lyrics are much too violent!"

DOWN WITH MUSH, DOWN WITH LOVE!
UP WITH PUSH, UP WITH SHOVE!
DOWN WITH NEAT, DOWN WITH CLEAN!
UP WITH DIRT, UP WITH MEAN!

"I agree," said Mr. Grizzmeyer.

Mr. Honeycomb looked straight at the vice principal and said, "Are they any more violent than your school fight song?"

Mr. Grizzmeyer sighed and shook his head. "I'm afraid he's right, Miss Glitch," he said. "We'll just have to approve them."

The other groups' lyrics passed without objections. All three grownups commented on how sweet the Jugsters' song of heartbreak was. It was the exact opposite of rude and crude, they said. But they also agreed that the Jugsters didn't stand a chance now that the contest would be judged by Stevie Sludge.

Chapter 11
A Shye Visitor

On the day of the contest, something unexpected happened. Something that put the chances of the front runners in doubt.

Stevie Sludge was scheduled to arrive in Beartown on the afternoon train from Big Bear City. A school committee was organized to greet him at the station. It consisted of Teacher Bob, Miss Glitch, and

Too-Tall and the Smashers. The Too-Tall gang plastered welcome posters all over the station, and as the train pulled in they held up a huge banner showing Toxic Sludge in the middle of their guitar-smashing frenzy.

Lots of passengers got off the train, but none of them looked anything like Stevie Sludge. They were all just ordinary folks on business or returning home or visiting family and friends.

Finally there was only one bear left standing on the station platform. He was every bit as ordinary-looking as all the others had been. He wore a suit and tie and a pair of horn-rimmed glasses. After glancing this way and that, he started walking toward the welcoming committee.

"That *couldn't* be Stevie Sludge, boss!" Skuzz whispered to Too-Tall. "Or could it?"

"No way," Too-Tall whispered back.

"Better check, anyway," said Skuzz.

Too-Tall stepped toward the approaching visitor. "Er—Mr. Sludge?"

The visitor smiled. "Why, yes," he said. "Of course, that's just my stage name, son. My real name is Arnold Shye."

"*Arnold Shye?*" said Too-Tall.

"That's right," said the visitor. "With an *e.*"

Word spread quickly that Mr. Arnold Shye, alias Stevie Sludge, looked like a businessbear instead of a rock star. That made everyone wonder about the outcome of the contest. After all, if Toxic Sludge's rad, grungy act was "just an act," it wasn't so easy to predict how their lead singer would judge the contest.

And that wasn't the *only* unexpected event that happened that day....

Chapter 12
Lost and Found

It had been decided that Cyberpunk would perform first at the contest because it took so long to set up their equipment. So Cyberpunk had their moving crew take the equipment to Great Grizzly Hall and set it up on stage hours before the contest.

But when the group got to the hall shortly before the contest, they found the stage empty. As Ferdy and Trudy ran all

around the hall looking for the equipment, Harry wheeled up to Too-Tall, who was his best chess-playing buddy. "Hey, big guy," he said. "Did you see what happened to the computer stuff that was on the stage?"

Too-Tall said he had just gotten there and that the stage had been empty when he arrived. He would check with his gang.

Skuzz, Smirk, and Vinnie, who had all arrived earlier, were sitting in the back row of the hall with smug little smiles on their faces. Too-Tall was already suspicious.

"Hey, boss," said Skuzz as Too-Tall approached, "looks like our *main competitors* have a problem."

"Yeah," said Smirk. "Looks like they ain't gonna be able to perform."

Too-Tall put his hands on his hips and stared straight at Skuzz. "What do you suppose happened to that equipment?" he asked.

"I dunno," said Skuzz. "Maybe it got lost."

"Maybe it got lost *where?*" said Too-Tall, leaning down and putting his nose right in Skuzz's face.

Skuzz tried to slide down in his seat to get away. "Maybe in the supply room?" he said. "In the basement?"

"Yeah, boss," said Vinnie. "Maybe in the back right-hand corner. Behind the office supplies."

"You idiots!" hissed Too-Tall. "Harry's my best friend outside of the gang! And none of *you* can play chess! So the stuff got 'lost,' did it? Well, now it's gonna get *found!* Pronto!"

Skuzz dashed to the basement stairs. Moments later he reappeared, yelling that he'd found Harry's equipment in the supply room. Fortunately, with the gang's help, Cyberpunk was able to set up in time for the contest.

Chapter 13
Go Figure

Finally it was time for the big contest to begin. The great hall was packed. From the front row, Arnold Shye peered up at the stage through his horn-rimmed glasses. Flashbulbs went off as Teacher Bob announced the first band.

Cyberpunk's number went off without a hitch and got a huge ovation from the audience. The Stand-ups followed and got no laughs. Backstage, Fred said to Brother, "Well, they've honed the act to perfection."

"Yeah," said Brother, "and it still stinks!"

Girlz went next and got a pretty good hand. The Jugsters were next to last. They were really nervous at the start, mainly because there was some snickering in the audience when Teacher Bob announced

them. Too-Tall had been spreading the rumor—the *true* rumor—that Gramps and Gran were responsible for the jug band aspect of the Jugsters. How embarrassing! But soon they were really able to get into the song, and the audience liked it. Bonnie's singing was a hit. They finished to very warm applause from cubs and grownups alike.

Last came Too-Tall and the Smashers. As Brother had predicted, they smashed four plywood guitars to smithereens to open the act, and another four to close it. They got a big ovation.

As soon as the hall had quieted down, Arnold Shye climbed onto the stage and went to the microphone. He blinked at the audience through his thick glasses. He seemed as shy as his name.

"Well," he said finally, "it wasn't easy choosing a winner. In fact, there were *three*

groups that could have won the prize. But I've decided it should go to Cyberpunk for their innovative, futuristic, cutting-edge sound." When the applause died down, he added, "Not to mention their *really* cool equipment!" That got some more applause.

"But as I said," continued Shye, "there were two other groups that could have won. They were so good that I've decided to give them honorable mentions. The first honorable mention goes to the Jugsters for their excellent music-making and for their creative, original use of traditional jug band instruments in a country-rock format." Long applause. "The second honorable mention goes to Too-Tall and the Smashers for their superb imitation of Toxic Sludge." More applause.

"And finally," said Shye, "I'm pleased to announce a special bonus prize for the winner. My very own group, Toxic Sludge, will take Cyberpunk on tour as our opening act!"

That brought down the house. Bear Country School really *would* go platinum! Trudy dragged Ferdy out from the wings, and they shook Arnold Shye's hand and bowed to the cheering audience. Ferdy

showed no more emotion than a smug smile could express, but at least he didn't look bored for once. Harry McGill, on the other hand, was so excited that he sped out onto the stage and did a wheelie with his wheelchair.

Now the big contest was all over. The audience began to file out of Great Grizzly Hall. Cyberpunk rushed off to Arnold Shye's hotel to discuss the details of the tour with him. The other groups gathered on the stage for a last look at the vast hall before the lights were all switched off.

"You know," said Brother, "this has been pretty amazing. Who would have thought when we saw that first Musicale notice on the bulletin board, that all *this* would happen?"

"Yeah," said Bonnie. "That we'd get the school to turn the Musicale into a rock contest?"

"Or that Too-Tall would get Stevie Sludge to agree to judge the contest?" said Queenie.

"Or that Stevie Sludge would turn out to be Arnold Shye?" said Too-Tall.

"Or that he would give an honorable mention to a band called the Jugsters?" said Sister.

"Not to mention take Cyberpunk on tour!" said Fred.

It was true. No one could have predicted any of it. And yet, it had all happened.

Stan and Jan Berenstain began writing and illustrating books for children in the early 1960s, when their two young sons were beginning to read. That marked the start of the best-selling Berenstain Bears series. Now, with more than one hundred books in print, videos, television shows, and even Berenstain Bears attractions at major amusement parks, it's hard to tell where the Bears end and the Berenstains begin!

Stan and Jan make their home in Bucks County, Pennsylvania, near their sons— Leo, a writer, and Michael, an illustrator— who are helping them with Big Chapter Books stories and pictures. They plan on writing and illustrating many more books for children, especially for their four grand-children, who keep them well in touch with the kids of today.

J
FIC
BER

Berenstain, Stan,
  1923-

The Berenstain Bears
go platinum.

33910020382918
$11.99   Grades 3-4   11/14/1998

DATE			

001036   9836361